William John M. Rankine

A Memoir of John Elder

engineer and ship-builder

William John M. Rankine

A Memoir of John Elder
engineer and ship-builder

ISBN/EAN: 9783337399795

Printed in Europe, USA, Canada, Australia, Japan

Cover: Foto ©Andreas Hilbeck / pixelio.de

More available books at **www.hansebooks.com**

A

MEMOIR

OF

JOHN ELDER

ENGINEER AND SHIPBUILDER

BY

W. J. MACQUORN RANKINE

WILLIAM BLACKWOOD AND SONS

EDINBURGH AND LONDON

MDCCCLXXI

ADVERTISEMENT.

THE Author of this Memoir desires to express his grateful sense of obligation to the family, friends, and business connections of the late Mr ELDER, for the ample information which they have supplied to him, and for the documents to which they have given him access.

W. J. M. R.

GLASGOW UNIVERSITY, 1870.

CONTENTS.

APPENDIX.

MEMOIR OF JOHN ELDER.

THE earliest accounts of the family of Elder show it to have flourished in the county of Kinross, in the east of Scotland, during the sixteenth and seventeenth centuries. The leading branch of the family seems to have been that which possessed the estate of Arlarie, near the town of Milnathort. There are on record the names of two John Elders of Balbughtie, cadets of the family of Arlarie, one of whom lived in the sixteenth, and the other in the seventeenth century, both forefathers of the subject of this Memoir.

The line of his direct ancestors for nearly two centuries affords a remarkable example of a fact which is more common than is usually supposed— the hereditary transmission of skill and talent; for they all practised that art from which (as Fairbairn tells us) mechanical engineering has sprung — that

A

of the millwright — and were all remarkable for ability and success.

The first of those regarding whom we possess definite information was ALEXANDER ELDER, wright at Craigo, about two miles west of Milnathort, born towards the end of the seventeenth century. He married Marion Ireland. His son DAVID ELDER, born in 1724, was a wright at Little Seggie, in the same neighbourhood; and from note-books of his, which are still preserved, he appears to have been a man of talent and information, and to have possessed considerable knowledge of mathematical and mechanical science. He was cut off in 1756, at the early age of thirty-two, leaving, by his wife Ellen Henderson, three sons and three daughters. His eldest son, ALEXANDER, born at Little Seggie about 1748, carried on at that place, and afterwards at Milnathort, the same business. He married Elizabeth Morrison, by whom he had two sons and three daughters, and died at Milnathort in December 1823.

In his eldest son, DAVID ELDER, the talent of the race, handed down through so many generations, began to achieve public distinction. He was born at Little Seggie on the 7th of January 1784, and died at Glasgow on the 31st of January 1866, at the close of a vigorous old age, being then in his eighty-second year. A memoir of his life by Mr James R. Napier, in which full justice is done to his remarkable character and abilities, was published in the 'Transactions of the Institution of Engineers in Scotland' for 1865-66; and therefore it is sufficient now to recapitulate the leading events of his career only. He learned the practical part of his trade as an apprentice to his father, and its scientific principles by the private study of mathematical books during intervals of leisure.

In 1808 he succeeded to his father's business at Little Seggie, which he quitted a few years afterwards for Paisley; and in 1817 he removed to Glasgow, thus obtaining a wide field for the exercise of his knowledge and skill as a millwright and mechanical engineer. In 1821 he became manager of the works of Mr Robert Napier, which office he continued to hold until induced by advancing age to retire.

In 1812 he married Grace, daughter of Mr John Gilroy; and the subject of the present Memoir was their third son.

JOHN ELDER was born at Glasgow on the 8th of March 1824. His elementary education was obtained in the High School of Glasgow. It does not appear

that he applied himself to the study of the ancient
classics; but the result of his training in English
scholarship became manifest in after-life; for in
writing and speaking on those practical and scientific
subjects which he understood so well, he showed
himself master of a clear, concise, and energetic style
of expression.

In arithmetic and mathematics, he was a pupil of
Dr Connell, one of the most able and successful
teachers of the time; and here he at once gave
proofs of extraordinary talent and application, carrying off the principal prizes of the class.

In every branch of drawing—an art intimately
connected with mechanical science—he was a most
successful student.

The studies before mentioned constituted the principal part of his early school education. A constitu-
tion naturally delicate prevented him from deriving
the full benefit of his attendance at the High School
of Glasgow, and from pursuing his studies to any
considerable extent at a university. A short attendance at the class of civil engineering in Glasgow
College was all the university education he received.
He was fortunate in being educated under the eye
of his father, whose extensive information and high

capacity were devoted to the training of his son, and under whose judicious advice he prosecuted his private studies with that ardour which was so marked a characteristic of his later years. The scientific knowledge of which he gave proof in after-life was not only varied and extensive, but was complete and exact, and free from the defects in thoroughness and accuracy which often beset self-taught scholars.

To those who knew him well, and enjoyed the advantage of personal communication with him, it was manifest that his eminence was due not so much to teaching by others as to the fact that John Elder was that rare character—a man of genius; and therefore in a great measure independent of that external control and guidance which are necessary for the training of ordinary students. In other words, his mind was gifted with the faculty of subjecting itself to that systematic labour and discipline which has to be enforced in ordinary cases by academic authority, and with that strong and clear vision which gives the learner the power of finding his way through the mazes of science without a guide.

He acquired, as his father also had done, considerable knowledge and practical skill in music, especially that of the organ.

He served his apprenticeship of five years as an engineer in the works of Mr Robert Napier, under the direction of his father, working successively in the pattern-shop, moulding-shop, and drawing-office. He was then employed for about a year as a pattern-maker in the works of Messrs Hick at Bolton-le-Moors, and afterwards as a draughtsman on the works of the Great Grimsby Docks.

Before 1849 he returned to the works of Mr Napier to take charge of the drawing-office, a most important appointment.

In the summer of 1852, the firm formerly called Randolph, Elliott, & Co. of Glasgow, well known and of high standing as millwrights, was joined by Mr Elder as a partner, and undertook the business of marine engineering, which they had never practised before, and which they were now enabled to undertake through possessing a partner with a thorough knowledge of the principles and practice of that branch of applied mechanics. The firm from that time was known by the designation of "Randolph, Elder, & Co." until 1868; and subsequent to the retirement of the other partners, its name became at first "John Elder," and then "John Elder & Co."

About 1860 the firm added shipbuilding to the other branches of its business.

The career of Mr Elder as a marine engineer and shipbuilder is so closely connected with the application of the compound expansive steam-engine to the propulsion of ships, that it now becomes necessary to introduce into this Memoir a brief explanation of the principles of that class of steam-engines, and a summary of their history from the time of their first invention.

In every machine a certain quantity of energy, or power of doing work, is expended, in order that a certain amount of work may be done. In every machine, and under all circumstances, the whole work done is equal to the energy expended; but only part of that work is useful, the remainder being useless, so that the energy expended in doing it is wasted. For example, in a pumping steam-engine the useful work consists in raising, in a given time, a certain quanity of water to a certain height: the useless, or wasteful work, is that done in overcoming friction. The proportion which the useful work done bears to the energy expended is called the *efficiency*. In an absolutely perfect machine, the efficiency would be represented by unity—but no such machine exists; and in every actual machine, the efficiency is expressed by a fraction which falls short of unity by an amount corresponding to the energy that is wasted.

In a steam-engine there are several successive causes of waste of energy. In the first place, the whole of the energy which the fuel is capable of producing by its combustion is not communicated to the water in the boiler, but only a certain fraction of that energy, ranging in ordinary cases from six-tenths to eight-tenths: this fraction is the *efficiency of the boiler;* and the amount by which it falls short of unity corresponds to the heat lost by imperfect combustion, by conduction and radiation, and by the high temperature at which the furnace-gas escapes through the chimney.

Secondly, the whole of the energy which in the form of heat is communicated to the water in the boiler, so as to raise its temperature and convert it into steam, is not obtained in the form of mechanical work done by the steam in driving the piston. In fact, it has for some years been known, through the progress of the science of thermodynamics, that the work done by the steam in driving the piston (often called the *indicated work,* because its amount can be registered by a self-acting instrument called the indicator) corresponds to a quantity of energy which has

disappeared from the form of heat, being the difference between the heat brought by the steam from
the boiler, and the heat carried away by the same
steam when it leaves the cylinder. That difference,
in every case which can occur in practice, is but a
small fraction of the whole heat brought by the steam
from the boiler, such as a twentieth, or a tenth; and
that fraction is the *efficiency of the steam.*

Thirdly, the whole of the energy exerted by the
steam in driving the piston is not communicated to
the machine which it is the purpose of the engine to
drive; for a fraction of that energy, say from an
eighth to a fourth, is wasted in overcoming the friction of the engine—the difference between that fraction and unity being the *efficiency of the mechanism.*

Fourthly, when the machine which it is the purpose of the engine to drive is an instrument for pro-
pelling a ship, a fraction of the energy is wasted in
agitating the water in which the propeller works, the
remainder only being usefully expended in overcoming the resistance of the vessel, and driving her ahead;
and the ratio which this last remainder bears to the
whole energy expended by the engine in driving the
propeller is a fraction called the *efficiency of the propeller.*

The efficiency of the whole combination, made up

of furnace, boiler, engine, and propeller, is found by multiplying together the four fractions already mentioned—viz., the efficiency of the boiler, the efficiency of the steam, the efficiency of the mechanism, and the efficiency of the propeller—and is of course a smaller fraction than any of the factors of which it is the product.

The object of improvements in the economy of the marine steam-engine is to increase as far as practicable, consistently with due regard to economy in first cost, each of the four factors of the efficiency.

Judgment, as well as skill, is specially required in applying to practice in marine steam-engineering improvements whose objects are to increase the mechanical efficiency of the furnace and boiler, of the steam in the cylinder, and of the mechanism; for those improvements for the most part tend more or less to increase the cost of construction; and thus there arises in each case the commercial question, Whether the economy in working to be attained by means of a given increase of efficiency is sufficient to warrant the additional expenditure? In deciding that question, regard must be had to many different circumstances—such as the length of the voyage, the intended speed, the price of fuel, and the nature of the traffic. For example, it would be a waste of money and labour to make elaborately-designed boilers and engines of very high efficiency for vessels intended to run short trips between places where coal is cheap and abundant; while for ships designed to make long voyages, with few and distant coaling stations, and expensive fuel, every improvement that increases efficiency may be a profitable investment. It is not sufficient, then, for success in the business of marine engineering, that the engineer should possess knowledge of the mechanical principles of his art, and skill in their practical application—for these qualifications alone might lead him into needless expense in the production of a degree of mechanical efficiency not required by the circumstances of particular cases; he ought also to have a sound judgment regarding the commercial result of the adaptation of engines of a given kind to a given vessel, intended for a given trade.

Those different qualifications are so seldom found united in one man, that the tendency of popular opinion is to regard them as incompatible, and to look especially upon the knowledge, skill, and enterprise which lead an engineer to adopt new or unusual improvements in practice as being fraught with danger to his success in business; and so no doubt they are, unless regulated by commercial sagacity.

The success of Mr Elder and of his firm proved
that his commercial sagacity was not inferior to his
knowledge, skill, and enterprise, and that his was
one of those rare minds in which was realised that
uncommon combination of talent.

It now becomes necessary to point out more in
detail the nature of the improvements which Mr
Elder, by himself, or with the co-operation of his
firm, carried out in the practice of marine engineering; and as the most important of these were
connected with the second and third factors of efficiency already referred to—that of the steam in its
action on the piston, and that of the mechanism—
the circumstances on which that second factor depends will, in the first place, be explained.

The expenditure of energy in the form of heat
required in order to produce a given weight of steam,
when the water is supplied to the boiler at a given
temperature, increases when the pressure and temperature of the steam increase, but at a comparatively slow rate. For example, the expenditure of
heat required to produce a given weight of steam at
the pressure of *ten atmospheres* (about 147 lb. on
the square inch of absolute pressure, or 132.3 lb.
on the square inch above the atmosphere), the feed-
water being at the temperature of about 100° Fahren-

heit, is greater than that required to produce an
equal weight at the atmospheric pressure, in the
proportion only of 1.04 to 1, or 26 to 25 nearly.
Hence the problem of obtaining the greatest possible
quantity of indicated work from a *given expenditure
of heat* in producing steam, is so nearly identical
with that of obtaining the greatest possible quantity
of work *from a given weight of steam*, that in practice
the difference between those two problems may be
neglected.

All mechanical work is done by the exertion of
a force through a space, and is calculated and expressed as a quantity by multiplying the mean
amount of the force into the space through which
it acts. In the case of steam, the space is the distance through which the piston is driven in a given
time; the force is the excess of the forward pressure
exerted by the steam behind the piston as it comes
from the boiler, and afterwards expands, above the
backward pressure exerted by the steam in front of
the piston while it is being expelled from the cylinder into the condenser in condensing engines, or into
the atmosphere in non-condensing engines. In a
non-condensing engine the back-pressure is a little
greater than that of the atmosphere, say from 15 lb. to
18 lb. on the square inch. In a condensing engine

the back-pressure is lower than that of the atmosphere, to an extent depending on the efficiency with which the condenser acts (or on the goodness of the vacuum, as it is commonly called), and ranges in ordinary cases from 3 lb. to 5 lb. on the square inch.

In an expansive steam-engine, the forward pressure exerted by the quantity of steam that is admitted behind the piston at each stroke has two stages in its action—the admission and the expansion. During the admission the steam is coming from the boiler into the cylinder, and it exerts a pressure less than that in the boiler only by the amount required to overcome the friction of pipes, passages, and valve-ports: say about a twelfth of the absolute pressure in the boiler in ordinary cases. The admission is terminated by the cut-off—that is, by the closing of the valve which admits the steam into the cylinder. Then follows the expansion of the steam which is confined in the cylinder; and during this stage of its action, it goes on occupying a continually increasing space as it drives the piston before it, and exerting a continually diminishing pressure. The exact law according to which the pressure diminishes while the steam expands is complicated, and is different under different circumstances as to heat. For ordinary practical calculations, however, it is sufficiently accurate to assume the simple approximate law that the pressure varies inversely as the volume, falling to one-half of its original intensity when the volume is doubled, to one-third when the volume is trebled; and so on.

It is obvious that work continues to be done by the steam in driving the piston so long as the pressure behind the piston, or forward pressure, continues to be greater than the pressure in front, or back-pressure, exerted by the steam which has already done its work, and which the piston is expelling from the cylinder; and hence it follows, that in order to realise the greatest quantity of work which the steam is capable of performing, the expansion ought to be carried on until the forward pressure of the steam behind the piston has fallen so low as to be just sufficient to overcome the back-pressure, and that to end the expansive working of the steam at an earlier period of the stroke is to throw away part of the power of the steam.

This statement must, however, be taken with the qualification that when the excess of the forward pressure above the back-pressure falls below the pressure which is just sufficient to overcome the friction, the work done is no longer partly useful and partly wasteful, but is wholly wasteful; whence it follows that, although in order to obtain the greatest *indicated* work from a given weight of steam the expansion should be continued until the forward pressure becomes just equal to the back-pressure, the greatest *useful* work is obtained by making the expansion cease when the forward pressure is just equal to the back-pressure added to a pressure equivalent to the friction of the engine.

Another obvious principle is, that both the indicated and the useful work obtained from a given weight of steam must be the greater the greater the proportion in which the forward pressure exceeds the back-pressure. To take an extreme case: If the mean forward pressure be simply equal to the back-pressure, no indicated work whatsoever is obtained from the steam; and if the mean forward pressure is simply equal to the back-pressure added to the friction, no useful work is obtained. Hence the higher the forward pressure, and the lower the back-pressure, the greater is the efficiency of the steam in an engine; and as the pressure increases and diminishes with the temperature, the same principle may be otherwise expressed by saying that the temperature of the steam on its admission ought to be as high as possible, and that in a condensing engine the temperature in the condenser, on which the back-pressure depends, ought to be as low as possible. In a non-condensing engine, the back-pressure, as formerly stated, is a little above that of the atmosphere.

The foregoing principle, as applied to the temperature in a condensing engine, was first distinctly stated by James Watt; and he invented the separate condenser as a means of carrying it into effect.

The pressure at which the steam is admitted is limited only by the strength and safety of the boiler. In Watt's time, he, in common with most other engineers, was very cautious in the use of high pressures; and he therefore relied more on a low back-pressure than on a high forward pressure for the efficiency of his engines. Improvements in the construction of boilers, and experience of their safety under high pressures when properly designed and managed, have caused subsequent engineers to become gradually bolder in the use of such pressures.

In order to realise the greatest theoretical efficiency in the expansive working of steam, the expansion ought to take place in a non-conducting cylinder, with a non-conducting piston. This condition cannot be absolutely realised in practice; but means may be taken to diminish the loss of efficiency arising from the conducting power of the cylinder and piston until it becomes unimportant.

B

If that loss arose solely from the waste of heat by
its passage through the metal of the cylinder to the
air outside, it would be sufficient for its practical pre-
vention to clothe the cylinder with bad conductors,
such as wood and felt. But by far the greater part
of that loss arises in a different and more complex
way, which was not thoroughly understood until
about 1849 or 1850, when the consequences of the
disappearance of heat in performing mechanical
work were demonstrated. Until that time it was
erroneously believed, from reasoning based on the
hypothesis of caloric, that a given weight of steam,
after performing work by expansion, contained exactly as much heat as before, and was therefore
superheated; because the quantity of heat sufficient
to keep it in the vaporous state at the higher pressure was more than sufficient to produce the same
effect at the lower pressure; and that statement was
so confidently believed that it was distinctly laid
down as a fundamental principle in all, or almost
all, writings on the theory of the steam-engine.

One of the earliest consequences deduced from the
principles of thermodynamics was, that when steam
performs work by expansion, a quantity of heat disappears sufficient not only to lower the temperature
of the steam to that corresponding to its lowered

pressure, but to cause a certain portion of the steam to pass into the liquid state. The steam thus spontaneously liquified collects in the form of water in the cylinder; and if the cylinder and piston were made of a non-conducting material, that water would simply be discharged from time to time into the condenser, without causing any waste of heat. But the cylinder and piston, being made of a conducting material, give out heat to the liquid water which adheres to them, so as to re-evaporate it when the communication with the condenser is opened; and that heat is carried off to the condenser with the exhaust-steam, leaving the piston and the inside of the cylinder at a low temperature, even though the outside of the cylinder should be clothed with an absolute non-conductor. When steam from the boiler is admitted at the beginning of the next stroke, part of it is immediately liquified through the expenditure of its heat in raising the piston and the inside of the cylinder again to a high temperature, the result being that at the end of the second stroke the quantity of liquid water which is re-evaporated, and carries off heat to the condenser, is greater than it was at the end of the first stroke. At each successive stroke that quantity augments until it reaches a fixed amount, depending mainly on the difference of the temperatures of the steam at the beginning and end of the expansion; and the effect is the same as if a certain quantity of steam at each stroke passed directly from the boiler to the condenser without performing work. In some experiments lately made, the quantity of steam which thus ran to waste was found to be greater than that which performed work; so that the expenditure of steam was more than doubled.

The remedy for this cause of loss is to prevent that spontaneous liquifaction of the steam during its expansive working, in which the process just described originates ; and that is done either by enclosing the cylinder in a *jacket* or casing supplied with hot steam from the boiler, or by superheating the steam before its admission into the cylinder; or by both those means combined. The steam is thus kept in a nearly dry state, so as to be a bad conductor of heat ; and the moisture which it contains, though sufficient to lubricate the piston, is not allowed to increase to such an extent as to carry away any appreciable quantity of heat from the metal of the cylinder and piston to the condensers.

The steam-jacket outside the cylinder was invented and used by Watt. Whether he fully understood the nature of its action can never be known ; for he did not publish any reason for using it except

that of keeping the steam as hot as possible. Its
real action was certainly not understood by Watt's
immediate successors, nor indeed by any one, until
the principles of thermodynamics were applied to
the question about twenty years ago; and many
engineers, reasoning correctly from the erroneous hypothesis of caloric, concluded that the steam-jacket
was unnecessary, and abandoned its use. The fact of
liquid water collecting in the cylinder was known,
but was ascribed to "priming," or the carrying of
spray from the boiler. The use of the steam-jacket
was retained in a few special kinds of engines, such
as the Cornish pumping-engines; and in them the
economy properly due to high rates of expansion of
the steam was realised; but in almost all other
engines, and certainly in marine engines, the jacket
was abandoned, with this result—that little or no
practical advantage was found to result from expansive working when the steam was expanded to more
than about double, or two and a half times its original
volume; and this became a received maxim amongst
engineers, and especially amongst marine engineers,
for its truth in the case of unjacketed cylinders was
established by practical experience, as well as by
experiments made for the purpose of testing it.

The jacketing of the piston, by filling its internal

hollow with hot steam from the boiler, was invented by M. Normand of Havre, and introduced into Britain by Mr Davison at a comparatively recent date, after the action of the steam-jacket had been explained according to the principles of thermodynamics, and its use revived in practice.

So far as the theoretical action of the steam on the piston is concerned, it is immaterial whether the expansion takes place in one cylinder, or in two or more successive cylinders. The advantage of employing the compound engine is connected with those causes which make the actual indicated work of steam fall short of its theoretical amount, and also with the strength of the engine and its framing, the steadiness of its action, and the friction of its mechanism.

The force exerted by the steam on the piston of an engine is transmitted by the piston-rod to the moving pieces of the machinery which it drives—such as the connecting-rod, crank, and crank-shaft; and by the bearings of the moving pieces it is transmitted to the framework. It produces straining actions on all those pieces, moving and fixed; and each of them must be made strong enough to bear safely the straining action produced, not by the mean or average force exerted by the steam, but by the greatest force. The mean force which the steam has to exert

on the piston depends on the power required to do
the work of the engine, and on the mean speed of
the piston ; and the greater the rate of expansion,
the greater is the inequality between the greatest
force and the mean force, and the stronger must the
engine be made. For example, when the steam is
expanded to twice its original volume, its pressure
during its admission is about once and a fifth its
mean pressure ; when to five times, its pressure during admission is about double of its mean pressure ;
and when to ten times, its pressure during admission
is about three times its mean pressure ; so that in
this last example, if the engine is single cylindered,
all parts of the mechanism and framing that are
strained by the force of the steam must be made
three times as strong as they would require to be in
an engine of the same power working without expansion. That additional strength involves not only
additional cost of construction, but additional friction, because of the greater size of the bearings ; and
thus the economy of power due to expansion is
partly neutralised.

It was to obviate this disadvantage in the use of
high rates of expansion that the earliest form of
compound steam-engine was contrived by Hornblower in 1781. That engine was single-acting, and

adapted to the pumping of mines; it had two cylinders, standing side by side, and having their pistons
hung from the same end of the walking-beam; the
larger cylinder was of the dimensions suited for a
single-cylinder engine of the same power and speed;
but instead of admitting the steam at its comparatively high initial pressure to act upon the large area
of the piston of that cylinder, and thus to exert a
great straining force, it was admitted in the first
place into the smaller cylinder, so as to exert a
straining force equal to the initial pressure multi-
plied by the area of the smaller piston only; and
after having done part of its work by expansion in
the smaller cylinder, it was transferred to the larger
cylinder in a state of increased volume and dimi-
nished pressure to complete its action there. The
cylinders were called the high-pressure and low-
pressure cylinders respectively, and the same terms
are still used in describing compound engines.

The same principle of action was applied by
Woolf to engines with Watt's separate condenser,
and to double-acting steam-engines; and consequently compound engines came to be very generally
known as "Woolf's engines."

In Woolf's form of the compound engine, as well
as in Hornblower's, the two piston-rods are hung

from the same end of a walking-beam, so that the forces exerted through them act in the same direction at the same time; and the straining actions produced on the framing and mechanism are those due to the sum of those forces. The same is the case in those forms of direct-acting compound engines for marine purposes in which the high and low pressure piston-rods are hung from one cross-head. Hence, although the straining actions of the two rods are, in a well-designed engine of the construction just mentioned, less than in a single-cylindered engine of equal power, they are not so small as they may be made to become by causing the straining actions due to the two forces to oppose each other. This improvement, so far as the straining actions on a walking-beam and its bearings are concerned, was introduced by M'Naught, who hung the two piston-rods from the opposite arms of the walking-beam, so as to make the difference, instead of the sum of their straining forces, act on the main centre. The sum, however, of those forces still acts on the bearings of the shaft in M'Naught's engine, in the direct-acting engines already referred to, and in the forms of compound engine described in Mr Craddock's treatise on that subject. That book was published in 1847, and contains the descriptions and drawings of compound engines adapted to marine, locomotive, and other purposes, as patented by him at different times from 1840 to 1846.

Craddock's compound engine, as described by him in the treatise just mentioned, is direct-acting. The high and low pressure cylinders, placed side by side, are not exactly parallel to each other, but make a small angle in order to enable the engine to " pass the centre." The two piston - rods are connected with one crank; upon which, therefore, and upon the shaft and its bearings, they exert a straining action due to the resultant of their forces, which, though not quite, is very nearly equal to their sum.

Craddock's compound engine, as described in his treatise, is further defective through the absence of steam-jackets, which are now known to be essential to the realising of the economy properly due to high rates of expansion; and unless that economy be fully realised, the additional cost and complexity of a compound engine are thrown away.

It is true that in some steamers fitted with Craddock's engines, or engines resembling them, at a later date (viz., in 1858 and subsequently) the straining actions of the pistons were opposed to each other, and the cylinders were jacketed; but this was long after the time at which the proper principles of the construction of compound marine engines had been brought into practical use by Messrs Randolph, Elder, & Co.

In 1850 a peculiar form of compound steam-engine called the " continuous expansion engine " was patented by Mr Nicholson. The pistons of the high and low pressure cylinders drive two cranks at right angles to each other; and the straining action is the resultant of those due to the forces acting through the two rods. This form has considerable advantages in certain cases; but it was not brought into practical use till about six or seven years later.

It results, then, from the history of marine steam engineering, that previous to the formation of the firm of Randolph, Elder, & Co., the compound steam-engine had not been successfully applied in Great Britain to the propulsion of vessels; that compound engines such as Craddock's had been proposed for that purpose, but had not been designed so as fully to realise the advantages of that form of engine; that the abandonment of the steam-jacket in the practice of almost all marine engineers had made it useless, if not wasteful, to employ those high rates of expansion to which the compound engine is suited; and that as this practical error originated in an erroneous theory of the mechanical action of heat, founded on the hypothesis of substantial caloric, then universally prevalent, it was not to be expected that it should be reformed except by an engineer who had studied and understood the principles of the then almost new science of thermodynamics.

Such an engineer was Mr Elder. He knew, in common with other practical men, the fact that when high rates of expansion were used with a view to economy of fuel, their economical action was defeated by the gathering in the cylinders of large quantities of liquid water, which evaporated when the exhaust-port opened, and carried away heat to the condenser; but he had learned also—what was known to very few practical men fifteen years ago—that the formation of that liquid water originated in the disappearance of heat during the performance of work by the expansion of the steam, and that the remedy was to supply the cylinder with additional heat to replace that which so disappears, by returning to the practice of Watt and the Cornish engineers, and resuming the use of the steam-jacket.

Mr Elder had also mastered a subject which, before his time, had been almost wholly neglected, and which even now does not always meet with the attention that it deserves, and that is, the diminution of the friction of the engine by causing the forces which drive the shaft round to balance and neutralise, as far as possible, each other's actions on the bearings where the friction takes place. As an elementary illustration of this subject, suppose that a shaft is made to rotate by means of a single force applied to a single crank-pin. The whole of that force will be transmitted to the bearings, and will there produce a pressure which will cause a certain amount of friction in addition to that produced by the weight of the shaft. But if we now divide the force required to drive the shaft into two equal forces of half the amount, and apply them in opposite directions to a pair of cranks exactly opposite to each other, those two driving forces will balance each other as regards pressure on the bearings, and the friction will be that due to the weight of the shaft alone. It is impossible in practice to realise this balance of driving forces with absolute precision, but an approach to it can always be made. One of the most important advantages of compound cylinder engines with opposite cranks is their enabling that balance of driving forces to be approximately realised; and that advantage had been neglected or very imperfectly developed before Messrs Randolph, Elder, & Co. constructed their marine engines, which in this respect were a great improvement upon all compound engines previously invented.

The careful attention which Mr Elder had bestowed on the friction of engines and the means of diminishing it, is fully shown in an unpublished lecture which he delivered before the United Service Institution in April 1866. He there takes a practical example of a marine engine, and shows by detailed calculation how from 10 to 15 per cent of the whole indicated power of an engine may be wasted in unnecessary friction through neglect of proper arrangements for the mutual balancing of the forces exerted on the shaft. In fact, he took a more correct view of the real advantages of the compound engine than had previously been done by any practical engineer; regarding it as a means, not so much of increasing the indicated power produced by a given expenditure of steam, as of diminishing that waste of power which causes the effective power to fall short of the indicated power.

In the lecture already referred to, Mr Elder points out under what circumstances it becomes advantageous to employ a compound engine rather than a single-cylinder engine—viz., when the rate of expansion exceeds four. He adds that, should rates of expansion greater than nine be used, it will become advisable to expand the steam in three successive cylinders instead of two.

Most of the improvements introduced by Messrs Randolph, Elder, & Co. in marine engineering were secured by a series of patents, of which the following is a summary—the patents being distinguished by letters ; and it is also shown which of those patents were taken in the names of both partners, and which in the name of one only.

A. Charles Randolph and John Elder—dated 24th January 1853. An arrangement of compound engines adapted to the driving of the screw-propeller. The engines are vertical, direct-acting, and geared. The pistons of the high and low pressure cylinders move in contrary directions, and drive diametrically opposite cranks, with a view to the diminution of strain and friction.

B. John Elder—dated 28th February 1854. For an improved arrangement of the parts of horizontal direct-acting condensing engines for screw-steamers.

C. Charles Randolph and John Elder—dated 15th March 1856. This describes an arrangement of compound engines which was applied with most successful results to a long series of steamers. There are two diametrically opposite cranks and four cylinders, making a pair of compound engines ; the high and low pressure cylinder of each engine lie side by side in an inclined position, and their pistons move in contrary directions; and this arrangement not only promotes the balance of driving forces, but enables the steam to pass from the high pressure to the low pressure cylinder in the most direct manner possible, without having to traverse long crooked passages as it did in Hornblower's and Woolf's engines.

The directions in which the cylinders of the two engines lean are contrary—that is to say, for example, in a paddle-wheel steamer the forward engines incline backwards, and the after engines forward; and in a screw-steamer the starboard and port engines lean respectively to starboard and to port, so that their piston-rods make with each other an angle which, in different engines, ranges from 60° to 90°. The whole arrangement is one of the most simple and compact that is possible in a pair of compound engines, and it produces as near an approach to a balance of driving forces as is practicable when each engine has two cylinders only.

An ingenious contrivance for reversing the engine is described, consisting in an arrangement of epicyclic gearing, whereby a loose eccentric is made when required to overrun the shaft until it reaches the position for backward gear.

The specification fully states the importance of providing each cylinder with a steam-casing or jacket to prevent liquifaction: but this is not claimed; for it was not a new invention, but, as has been already explained, the revival of a practice which had fallen into neglect, though essential to the economical use of high rates of expansion.

D. John Elder—dated 29th January 1858. The specification of this patent describes an arrangement of cylinders in the compound engine by which a nearly perfect balance of driving forces is obtained, and not merely a good approximation to such balance, as in the arrangements previously described; and consequently it may be regarded as embodying the principles of the construction of steam-engines of which Mr Elder approved, in their most complete form, calculated to realise the greatest possible efficiency of the mechanism as well as of the steam. There are three cranks on the shaft—two pointing diametrically opposite to the third, which lies between them. Each engine has three cylinders, lying parallel to each other and side by side; in the middle is the high-pressure cylinder, whose piston drives the middle crank; at its two sides are a pair of low-pressure cylinders, whose pistons move simultaneously in the contrary direction to that of the middle cylinder, and drive the other two cranks. Thus the resultant of the forces exerted through the two low-pressure piston-rods is not merely contrary in direction, but directly opposed to the force exerted through the high-pressure piston-rod; and if the rates of expansion in the high and low pressure cylinders are properly adjusted to their dimensions, there is an exact balance of the actions of those forces on the bearings.

When there is only one low-pressure cylinder, as in the engines described under patent *C*, the forces exerted through the two piston-rods may be equal and contrary, but they are not directly opposed, because they are exerted at different points in the shaft; and hence the balance of driving forces cannot be quite exact.

Two or more three-cylindered compound engines can be placed at suitable angles of inclination to each other, so as to drive one shaft, as in the arrangement of two-cylindered engines described in specification *C*.

As the three-cylindered compound engine is somewhat more expensive than a two-cylindered compound engine of the same power, it has been used only in certain cases where special economy of power was desired. Its success in practice will be described further on.

In specification *D*, as well as in specification *C*, the importance of the steam-jacket is mentioned; but, for the reason already stated, that part of the engine is not claimed.

E. John Elder—dated 7th June 1858. This patent is for a very simple but very important improvement —the making of paddle-floats of plates of iron or steel, bevelled to a sharp edge, instead of thick wooden planks. The broad edges of wooden paddle-floats oppose a resistance to the plunging them into and drawing them out of the water; and the inventor considered that the substitution for them of comparatively thin sharp-edged metal plates caused a gain of from 4 to 6 per cent in the speed of a given vessel with engines of a given power. This invention was perfectly successful in practice, and was applied to several steamers in the course of the year in which the patent was obtained, and it still continues to be put in practice by the firm with beneficial results.

F. Charles Randolph and John Elder—dated 28th April 1859. This patent is for a variety of improvements in engines and boilers, which it is unnecessary to describe in detail. Amongst other inventions, it describes the making of a boiler with two or more uptakes, in order to increase the surface for super-heating the steam.

G. John Elder—dated 15th October 1859. This patent relates to details of mechanism for moving slide-valves.

H. John Elder—dated 25th April 1862. This relates to a variety of improvements, amongst which may be mentioned improvements on slide-valves, so contrived as to give a smaller opening for the admission of steam and a larger for the exhaust; reversing-gear, in which the position of the eccentric is changed when required by the action of a spiral feather on a shaft which is capable of being shifted longitudinally; arrangements for working steam expansively in four successive cylinders; and an improved kind of water-tube boiler.

I. Charles Randolph and John Elder—dated 20th April 1863. Improvements in surface-condensers, provisionally protected only.

J. John Elder — dated 18th November 1863. This patent is for constructing plate-iron floating-docks, so as to be capable of being navigated from place to place by sails and steam. Three such floating-docks were built by the firm, but were not navigated: one was for Java; another for the French Government, fitted up at Saigon, in Cochin-China; the third was for a company in Peru. The two latter have been of great service, and are at present in successful operation.

K. John Elder — dated 19th November 1863. This patent is for various modifications in compound engines, and amongst others for a convenient arrangement of the surface-condenser, in which it is divided into two parts, with tubes parallel to the screw-propeller shaft.

L. John Elder—dated 9th July 1866. This also is for modifications of compound engines.

M. Charles Randolph—dated 15th December 1866. This relates to hydraulic or water-tube propellers.

N. John Elder — dated 28th September 1867. For improvements in floating-batteries—a most remarkable and important invention, which will be described further on.

The first vessel fitted with compound engines by Messrs Randolph, Elder, & Co., was the screw-steamer Brandon. Her engines were of the kind described in specification *A*. She made her trial-trip in July 1854, when her rate of consumption of coal was found to be about $3\frac{1}{4}$ lb. per indicated horse-power per hour. It is well known that the lowest rate of consumption of coal in steamers previous to that time was about 4 lb. or $4\frac{1}{2}$ lb. per indicated horse-

power per hour; and such, indeed, is the greatest
economy that can be expected from such rates of
expansion of the steam as are suitable for unjacketed
cylinders.

The Brandon was chartered during the Crimean
war as a despatch - boat, and maintained during
many years of service the same economy which she
had realised on her trial.

The second and third ships were the paddle-
steamers Inca and Valparaiso, for the Pacific Steam
Navigation Company. The engines of the Inca
were started in May 1856, those of the Valparaiso
in July 1856. Each of these ships had a pair of
engines of that compound class described in patent
C, already mentioned; the cylinders were jacketed
at top and bottom only, and not round the sides.

The first ship in which engines of the same
kind had their cylinders completely jacketed was
the Admiral, built by Mr J. R. Napier, and engined
by Messrs Randolph, Elder, & Co. Her trial-trip
was made in June 1858; and in October 1858 she
was followed by the Callao, built by Messrs John
Reid & Co. of Port Glasgow. The rate of consump-
tion of coal was found to be: In the Inca, $2\frac{1}{2}$ lb.; in
the Valparaiso and the Admiral 3 lb.; and in the
Callao 2.7 lb. per indicated horse-power per hour—a

degree of economy never before realised in marine engines; and this was not only obtained on the trial-trips, but maintained during many years' subsequent service at sea. It amounted to saving of from 30 to 40 per cent of the coal previously burned by steamers of the same class ; and it is not too much to say that it was this saving which rendered it practicable to carry on steam navigation on the Pacific Ocean with profit.

The success of the engines of those ships may be held to have conclusively established the practical value of the principles on which they were designed; and it was followed by the construction, by Messrs Randolph, Elder, & Co., of a long series of steamers, in which the same principles, being more fully carried out—that is to say, with higher initial pressures, greater rates of expansion, and greater proportions of superheating surface—realised even greater economy, the regular rates of consumption of fuel ranging from $2\frac{1}{2}$ lb. to $2\frac{1}{4}$ lb. per indicated horse-power per hour.

Another natural consequence was the adoption in the practice of other marine engineers of the same fundamental principles—that is to say, the use of high rates of expansion in the engines of vessels intended for long voyages, together with the means of causing such rates to realise their proper economy

—viz., jacketing and superheating. In carrying out these principles, different forms of engine have been designed by different engineers—some have devised peculiar forms of the compound engine, others have preferred that the whole work of the steam should be done in one cylinder. In some cases, forms of engine that had long before been proposed, but not executed, have been revived and applied to practice. The detailed history of all these inventions and improvements would be very interesting, but it would be foreign to the purpose of the present Memoir.

In 1865 a comparative trial was made by the Government of the performance of three kinds of marine engines, fitted in three of her Majesty's ships, the Arethusa, the Octavia, and the Constance. Those three vessels are of nearly similar model, and of nearly equal size—the tonnage of all three lying between 3100 and 3200 tons. Each vessel was fitted with engines of 500 nominal horse-power, and with surface-condensers.

There is no reason to believe that the engines of any one of those three ships were in the slightest degree inferior to those of the others in materials or execution, all three being in these respects of the very first order; and the comparison between them must therefore be regarded as showing how the efficiency of the boilers, engines, and mechanism was affected by the principles embodied in their respective designs.

The principal differences were in the construction of the mechanism of the engine. The Arethusa had a pair of single-cylindered direct-acting horizontal trunk-engines, with cranks at right angles, by Messrs John Penn & Sons.

The Octavia had a set of three single cylinders, horizontal and direct, with double piston-rods acting on three cranks, making with each other equal angles of 120 degrees. These were made by Messrs Maudslay.

The Constance had a pair of three-cylindered compound engines, of the construction designated by D in the account already given of Mr Elder's inventions, and described as giving the closest approximation to a balance of driving forces on the shaft. Thus the engines of the Arethusa had in all two cylinders, those of the Octavia three, and those of the Constance six.

Those three ships started together from Plymouth at six o'clock in the evening of the 30th September 1865, in order to run by the most direct course practicable to Funchal in Madeira, a distance of very nearly 1100 nautical miles.

For three days the three ships ran a nearly direct

course under steam alone, the Constance and the
Arethusa gaining slightly on the Octavia.

The Arethusa then made sail, and ran for three
days more under steam and canvas combined, her
course diverging to the eastward. During those
three days the Constance and the Octavia continued
to run a nearly direct course for Funchal, almost
wholly under steam alone, each of those two ships
having made sail for a few hours only. The Constance continued to gain on the Octavia.

On the 6th of October the Constance was 30 nautical miles from Funchal, 130 ahead of the Octavia,
and about 200 from the Arethusa—the last-named
ship being about 170 miles to the E.S.E. of the direct
course from Plymouth to Funchal.

In the course of the same day the engines of the
Arethusa and of the Octavia were stopped, as their
coal was nearly exhausted, and they ran nearly all
the rest of the way to Funchal under canvas alone,
making several tacks.

The engines of the Constance were eased on the
6th of October, because of a westerly gale and head
sea, and she arrived at Funchal on the 7th of
October at 3 P.M., the Octavia on the 9th at 6.45
A.M., and the Arethusa on the 10th at 5.35 P.M.

Considering that the last two vessels completed

the trip under sail and in stormy weather, it is obvious that no fair comparison between their engines and those of the Constance can be deduced from the *total* time occupied between Plymouth and Funchal. In the case of the Arethusa, too, her having been three days under steam and canvas combined makes it difficult, if not impossible, to form a satisfactory judgment of her comparative economy of power.

A comparison, however, though a rough one, of the three vessels, as regards the consumption of coal per indicated horse-power per hour, may be deduced from the official return published by the Admiralty of the power and of the fuel consumed from the 30th September to the 6th October, when the engines of the Arethusa and the Octavia were stopped, and those of the Constance eased. The following is the calculation, with its results :—

	Arethusa.	Octavia.	Constance.
Hours under steam, 30th Sept. to 6th Oct., inclusive,	134	140	124
Consumption of coal (tons),	228.85	276.74	242.5
Mean consumption per hour (tons),	1.71	1.98	1.96
Mean indicated power,	1052.2	1399.8	1747
Mean rate of consumption (lb.) per indicated horse-power per hour,	3.64	3.17	2.51

As regards the *efficiency of the mechanism*, the same return affords the means of comparing together in a general way the Octavia and the Constance, the Arethusa being excluded from the comparison because of her having run so long under canvas and steam combined. The principle upon which the comparison is based is, that in similar vessels of equal size, with mechanism of equal efficiency, the indicated power varies as the cube of the speed; and consequently, that if for two or more similar and equal vessels the cube of the speed of each vessel be divided by the indicated power, the proportions of the quotients to each other will show the comparative efficiency of the mechanism in the different vessels. The following is the calculation for the Octavia and the Constance, with results :—

	Octavia.	Constance.
Time under steam, ...	140	124
Distance run (nautical miles), . .	1051.7	1090.7
Mean speed (knots), ...	7.52	8.80
Cube of speed (omitting fractions), . .	425	682
Indicated power, do., . .	1400	1747
Quotients, ...	0.304	0.39
Proportionate efficiency of mechanism, .	100 :	127
Or, .	79 :	100

This may otherwise be expressed by saying, that at the same speed the Octavia would require 27 per cent more indicated power than the Constance, or the Constance 21 per cent less power than the Octavia. This comparison is not to be considered as very precise, because, strictly speaking, it is the mean value of the cube of the speed, and not the cube of the mean speed, that should be divided by the indicated horse-power.

The superior economy of fuel, as compared with indicated power, in the Constance is, of course, to be accounted for by a higher initial pressure and a greater rate of expansion than those used in the other vessels, combined possibly with better jacketing and greater superheating. But the superiority of the Constance over the Octavia in efficiency of mechanism—in other words, in economy of indicated power as compared with effective power—can be accounted for only by the comparative smallness of the friction in the engines of the Constance; and when it is considered that the engines of the Octavia were of a good design and of the best possible workmanship, the comparative smallness of the friction in the Constance must be ascribed mainly, if not wholly, to the balance of driving forces—the result of the arrangement of cylinders and cranks in Mr Elder's three-cylindered compound engines.

In a previous series of comparative trials of the Octavia and the Constance, each of those vessels made a run of 100 miles at each of the three speeds of 6, 8, and 10 knots, with the following results :—

	Octavia.	Constance.
Rate of consumption of coal per indicated horse-power per hour—		
At six knots, ...	1.90	2.31
At eight knots, ...	2.16	1.95
At ten knots, ...	2.58	2.11
Mean of the three trials, ...	2.21	2.12
Indicated horse-power—		
At six knots, ...	500	399
At eight knots, ...	1247	1046
At ten knots, ...	1633	1483

Proportionate efficiency of mechanism—

At six knots, ...	$\left\{\begin{matrix}\end{matrix}\right.$	100 :: 80	: :	125 100
At eight knots, ...	$\left\{\begin{matrix}\end{matrix}\right.$	100 :: 84	: :	119 100
At ten knots, ...	$\left\{\begin{matrix}\end{matrix}\right.$	100 :: 91	: :	110 100
Mean, ...	$\left\{\begin{matrix}\end{matrix}\right.$	100 :: 86	: :	115 100

During this series of comparative trials, the two ships appear to have been nearly equal in economy of fuel for a given indicated power. The superiority of the Constance in the efficiency of the mechanism, though smaller than that deduced from the report of the trip to Funchal, is still sufficient to prove a great diminution of friction through the balance of driving forces in the three-cylindered compound engine, and thus to furnish another practical proof of the soundness of Mr Elder's views respecting the waste of power in the friction of engines, and the means of diminishing that waste.

Although Mr Elder invented certain forms of boiler applicable under special circumstances, he did not confine the practice of his firm to any peculiar form, but adapted the boilers to the service for which the vessel was intended. His opinion on this point is summed up in the following quotation from the lecture already referred to : " A judicious engineer will therefore design different forms of boilers for different circumstances, the object being to construct all his work so as to give the best return to the capitalist that employs him."

On the whole, however, he used cylindrical boilers, fired at both ends, more frequently than other forms, and latterly he used this form alone.

The same remark applies to superheaters. The form of superheater which he generally employed consisted of an uptake passing through the steam-chest; and he varied the extent of superheating surface according to the degree of economy to be aimed at.

As regards condensation, he approved of the ordinary jet-condenser for fresh-water navigation, and for trips of moderate length in salt water.

For long sea-voyages, his firm and he latterly

adopted the surface-condenser, as being more economical in working, though somewhat greater in first cost; nevertheless, the remarkable economy of fuel in the earlier compound engines made by the firm was attained without the aid of surface-condensation.

The power of calculating beforehand the probable engine-power required in order to drive a given ship at a given speed, or the probable speed at which a given ship will be driven by a given amount of engine-power, is obviously of much practical value.

It has long been well known that at moderate speeds the engine-power required to drive a given ship varies nearly as the cube of the speed.

About 1844 Mr Scott Russell discovered the law that regulates the limits within which that principle is approximately true—viz., the speed must not exceed that with which a wave naturally travels whose length bears certain fixed proportions to the lengths of the entrance and run of the vessel; for so soon as the speed exceeds that limit, the power required begins to increase more rapidly than the cube of the speed. Hence a *moderate speed* for a given vessel may be understood to mean a speed not exceeding the limit determined by applying Mr Scott Russell's principle to that vessel. A speed exceeding that limit may be called an excessive speed.

Early in 1858, an investigation of the laws of the resistance of ships, based on experiment and observation, was made by the author of this Memoir at the instance of Mr J. R. Napier, who required it for practical purposes in shipbuilding ; and it led to the result that at *moderate speeds*, in the sense before mentioned, the resistance is chiefly of the kind called skin-resistance, depending on the friction between the water and the immersed surface of the ship, and that the power required to drive her may be calculated approximately by multiplying the cube of the speed by a constant factor depending on the roughness or smoothness of the skin, and by a quantity called the *augmented surface*, which depends on the areas of the various parts of the skin, and on their positions relatively to the course of the particles of water that glide over them—it being always understood, however, that the figure of the vessel must be such as to cause the particles to glide smoothly over her skin, and not to strike or dash against it, or become broken into eddies or foam.

The first ship to which those principles were applied, in order to calculate beforehand the power required at a given speed, was the paddle-wheel steamer Admiral, built by Mr J. R. Napier, and engined by Messrs Randolph, Elder, & Co., in 1858, as already mentioned; and the result was perfectly successful. The theory on which those principles were based, and the rules for applying them, were published in 1860. Mr Elder, with that ready appreciation of the practical value of scientific principles by which he was distinguished, at once made himself master of those principles, and continued afterwards to use them in estimating the probable power required in proposed vessels.

It has already been shown that Messrs Randolph, Elder, & Co. did not confine their practice to the construction of that form of compound engine which approaches the nearest to theoretical perfection, but adopted modified forms suited to the circumstances of particular cases. In addition to the instances already given, it may be mentioned that in many merchant screw-steamers, where simplicity of construction and fewness of parts were aimed at, they used a form of compound engine resembling that already mentioned as having been first proposed by Nicholson—a form which of late years has been adopted by many marine engineers. There are only two cylinders in all—a high-pressure cylinder and a low-pressure cylinder; they stand side by side, and their pistons drive two cranks at right angles to each other ; and there is an intermediate steam-reservoir, believed to have been first added to this kind of engine by Mr E. A. Cowper, into which the steam passes from the high-pressure cylinder before its admission into the low-pressure cylinder. In the engines of this kind made by Mr Elder, the reservoir forms an outer cylinder of the same diameter with the low-pressure cylinder, and surrounding the high-pressure cylinder, the whole arrangement being very compact and simple, though not having the same advantages in point of balance of driving forces and diminution of friction which are possessed in the highest degree by the engines described under Elder's patent *D*, and in a less degree by those described under Randolph and Elder's patent *C*.

There were cases in which, for the sake of still greater simplicity and compactness, it became advisable to dispense with compound engines and high rates of expansion, as not being required under the circumstances, and of such cases the following is an example.

Between 1861 and 1864, a demand arose for a class of cargo steamers of very shallow draught, capable of running at a very high speed, not for a great length of time, but on occasions of emergency. Five such vessels were built and engined by Messrs

Randolph, Elder, & Co. They were of a very fine model, driven by paddle-wheels, with feathering plate-iron floats, and each of them had a pair of single -cylindered oscillating engines of ordinary form. Their boiler-power was very great for their size, so as to provide the means of producing steam with great rapidity and of high pressure when required. All those vessels attained a speed of from 16¼ to 16½ knots on their trial-trips ; and that speed was not only realised at sea, but sometimes even exceeded. On one occasion, for example, when one of them was very hard pressed, the bold and skilful officer who commanded her succeeded, by an alteration of trim, in increasing her speed to 17 knots, and thus enabled her to escape from imminent danger.

The firm of Randolph, Elder, & Co. was dissolved by the expiration of the copartnery on the 30th of June 1868, having then existed for sixteen years. During that period the firm had made 111 sets of marine steam - engines, whose aggregate nominal horse-power amounted to 20,145 ; they had built 106 vessels, whose aggregate tonnage amounted to 81,326 ; and they had also constructed three floating-docks. After the dissolution of the partnership, the works were carried on by Mr Elder alone.

The following statement of the quantity of work executed during the time which elapsed from the dissolution of the partnership till the end of the year 1869, shows that the business had in fact become one of the greatest of its kind in the world : Number of sets of engines made, 18; aggregate nominal horse-power, 6110 ; number of vessels built, 14; aggregate tonnage, builders' measurement, 27,027.

The number of workmen employed in the engine-work and shipbuilding yard is about four thousand. Mr Elder took a strong and friendly interest in their comfort and wellbeing, and was regarded by them with corresponding respect and gratitude as an employer who was just and kind, as well as able. Amongst other acts of his for their benefit, he promoted, about half a year before his lamented death, the establishment of an accident fund, by undertaking to contribute to it in each month a sum equal to that which the workmen should raise by subscription amongst themselves, the result being that the income of the fund is about five hundred pounds a - year. It is managed by a committee partly appointed by the firm from amongst the foremen, partly elected by the workmen.

Besides the lecture to which reference has already

been frequently made, the views of Mr Elder on marine engineering are set forth in three papers, which were read respectively to the British Association at Leeds in 1858, at Aberdeen in 1859, and at Oxford in 1860, and printed in the Transactions of that body.

Another lecture, delivered by Mr Elder to the United Service Institution on the 25th of May 1868, and printed in their Journal, relates to a very remarkable invention, that of circular ships of war. His knowledge, to which reference has already been made, of the laws of the resistance of the water to the motion of vessels, led him to the inference that a ship with a hull of the form of a very flat segment of a sphere, like a floating saucer or watch-glass, would require little or no additional power to drive her at a moderate speed, beyond that which is required to drive at the same speed a vessel of equal displacement and of the ordinary form. He tested this conclusion by experiment on models of about five feet in diameter, and found it to be correct; and although at first sight it may seem paradoxical, its soundness will be understood when it is considered that the stream-lines, or lines of motion of the particles of water as they glide over the bottom of the vessel, are, in the case of a flat spherical segment, of a fine form, being either exactly or nearly arcs of circles of a radius equal to that of the sphere. Mr Elder proposed that a vessel of this form, protected by a belt of armour, and by a deck of sufficient strength, should carry a circular turret suitably armed with guns, and should be provided with a system of submerged propellers, either of the screw or of the hydraulic kind, so arranged as to drive her in any direction, and, when required, to make her turn about her centre, thus dispensing with the necessity for any separate means of making the turret rotate. The probabilities in favour of the success of this invention are so strong, that a trial of it on a practical scale is much to be desired.

Mr Elder was for four years a captain in the First Lanarkshire Artillery Volunteers; but the multiplicity of his business engagements at length made it impracticable for him to continue to hold that command.

In April 1869, at the annual meeting of the Institution of Engineers and Shipbuilders in Scotland for the election of office-bearers, Mr Elder was unanimously elected President of that body; and its members looked forward with intense interest to the opening address which he would have had to deliver at the commencement of the session 1869-70. But their hopes were never to be fulfilled ; for his health, which had never been robust, at last gave way, and he died in London on the 17th of September 1869, at the early age of forty-five.

He had been married on the 31st of March 1857 to Isabella, daughter of Alexander Ure, Esq. of Glasgow ; and for about three quarters of a year after his death, his business remained in the hands of that lady as sole proprietrix, and was carried on with undiminished success. It then passed into the hands of other partners, but it still continues to bear the honoured name of JOHN ELDER.

Thus far this Memoir has related chiefly to the intellectual powers and the professional career of its subject. It is not to be supposed, however, that his mental cultivation was limited to professional matters. He possessed a large and varied stock of information on most subjects of general interest ; and with his clear head and excellent judgment, it is certain that in whatsoever pursuit he had chosen for his main occupation, he must have risen to distinction. The moral qualities of his mind were of a not less high order than his intellectual powers. While firm of purpose and energetic for every good object, he was kind, generous, and liberal, and one of the most truthful, just, and honourable men that ever lived.

As regards the higher aspects of his character, the compiler of this Memoir is fortunately able to produce the testimony of one whose qualifications to speak on that subject are better than his own. The following pages are extracted from a letter of the Reverend Norman Macleod, D.D.

. . . . . .

"He was a member of my congregation, and I knew him well. I have seen him in all variety of outward circumstances — in the heyday of his strength, vigorous in mind and body; when suffering from a painful and lingering illness; when ministering to his venerated father on his deathbed, and to his admirable mother in her sorrow. I know what he was to his wife—loved more than all; and very many know, and never will forget, what he was as a friend; and the better I and others knew him, the more we admired and loved him.

"Mr Elder was truly a religious man. He was not a man of the slightest pretence in anything. He was far too sincere and truthful for *that*. Nor was he given to express, in any degree corresponding to their reality and depth, his feelings or affections, but was singularly calm, quiet, and undemonstrative. His religion was not, therefore, of that type which too commonly and very easily passes in society under the name, merely because certain opinions

are held, and certain stereotyped phrases and shib-
boleths are made use of. His religion was a *life*,
not confined to the church or to Sunday, but carried
out every day, in the family, in the counting-house,
in society, and in business, manifested in untarnished
honour, in the sweetest temper, in gentle words, and
in remarkable and most unselfish considerateness for
the feelings and the wants of others. Such a religion
as his was the result of head, heart, and conscience
dealing honestly with truth, and of a very simple
and genuine faith in the love to him and authority
over him of Jesus Christ. It was the deliberate choice
of a strong will, affected by a pure mind, quick conscience, and affectionate heart. His character told
upon every department of his workshop and building-yard. Every one, from the oldest to the youngest,
felt the presence of the man, and were influenced by
his goodness as much as by his genius. In visiting
the other day his great building-yard, one of his oldest
and most trustworthy men, speaking of him, said to
me: 'I never saw any one like him, nor expect to see
his like again! He was so just, so true, so kind to
every one. Every man trusted him, and knew that
he would do all that was possible to benefit them in
every respect. He had many plans for their good,
which, alas! he was not spared to carry out. I never
heard a rough or unkind word coming from his lips.'

" His funeral was one of the most impressive sights
I ever witnessed. The busy works south of the
Clyde were shut, forge and hammer at rest, and
silent as the grave. The forest of masts along the
river were draped in flags, lowered half-mast in sign
of mourning. A very army of workmen, dressed
like gentlemen, followed his body—column after
column. Respectful crowds lined the streets, as if
gazing on the burial of a prince ; and every one of
us, as we took the last look of his coffin and left
his grave, felt that we had left a friend behind us."

.   .   .   .   .

APPENDIX.

No. I.

Extracts from Letters of the Rev. W. G. Fraser.

LOOKING back on my brief interviews with Mr Elder, I always felt he was not, like the old philosopher, so absorbed in his mathematics as to forget more vital interests.

When speaking with me on religious subjects, in his own quiet, clear, flowing, and forcible way, about translating the *facts* of Christ's life into our own lives, the unmistakable impression was left on my mind that he was actually making this part of his own religion, in endeavouring to improve the temporal condition of those around him. Whatever he did for the bodily comfort of those under him, flowed, I have no doubt, from this living principle rising from the centre of his own spiritual being —a God-given and Christ-implanted principle in the soul, leading to imitation of Christ in doing good to the bodies of men.

One could not help feeling, in intercourse with Mr Elder on matters religious, that what he said was not merely from the unseen region of thought, not mere pro-

fession and assertion, but experimental from heart and
life. And judging only from conversations with him, in
ignorance of his mode of caring for his numerous workmen, I shall be disappointed if there is not some proof in
the record of his life of the justness of my impressions,
that he was one who had at heart the temporal good of
his workmen, and who wished this, as Christ wished to
fill the nets of those who had toiled all night without
success. In the spirit of the master, I should conclude,
that he carried out Paul's precept, "Be ye kind and
affectionate one to another."

Mr Elder, though always calm, seemed always cheerful,
never morose in conversation, sure to add some point or
line of light on the subject of discussion. He was one of
those "flowing light-fountains" of general knowledge, of
unostentatious Christian principle, as well as eminent
engineering skill—"a living light-fountain," which one
felt (when they had found it) was both pleasant and
profitable to abide under its radiance.

Had John Elder been spared to us, I am certain, from
the spirit that leavened his motives, from the power combined with gentleness which characterised him, that he
would have contributed large practical help in solving some
of the difficult problems that are so often springing up
between employers and employed in this country. I
remember, after his furlough in Russia, how he contrasted
the price of labour there with our higher prices here, and
how, in genuine sympathy with the working man, he
regretted those strikes as frequently far more injurious

and disastrous to the men than to the masters, and how
he wished to devise some plan whereby the men might
be saved the hardships of standing out so long, and trade
be prevented from leaving our shores, which it would ultimately do if strikes increased.

That Mr Elder had not only the temporal interests
of the men at heart, but also their highest moral and
spiritual interests, I feel certain, from the way in which
he spoke of their doubts in a conversation on the infi-
delity of the age, and the mode he counselled us and all
teachers to adopt in grappling with doubters; the apt
illustration being that of Thomas, the doubting disciple,
who did not at first believe that most vital and fundamental truth, the resurrection of the Lord Jesus. Yet
the Saviour did not frown upon him as an infidel, nor
sneer sarcastically at him, but came down and met him
on his own ground, as if he entered into his doubts, and
asked him to examine for himself the unmistakable proofs
of the *facts* of his resurrection; whereas, had Thomas
been treated coolly, and called hard names for doubting
what all the others believed, humanly speaking, he might
have turned away in confirmed unbelief.

The great Teacher, however, dealing sympathisingly
and gently with Thomas, led him, from unbelief to faith,
to exclaim, "My Lord, and my God." In like manner
(continued Mr Elder) we should endeavour to meet all
doubters on their own ground, giving them credit for
what they do believe, and striving to furnish evidence
for what they have difficulty about. In this way many

might be saved from the ranks of unbelief. Tennyson's lines in 'In Memoriam,' XCV., were partly quoted :—

> "Perplexed in faith, but not in deeds,
> At last he beats his music out;
> There lives more faith in honest doubt,
> Believe me, than in half the creeds.
> He fought his doubts and gathered strength ;
> He could not make his judgment blind ;
> He faced the spectres of the mind,
> And laid them : thus he came at length
> To find a stronger faith his own ;
> And power was with him in the night,
> Which makes the darkness and the light,
> And dwells not in the light alone."

．　．　．　．　．　．

Although it was my privilege and happiness to have those frequent interviews with Mr Elder, and although we had often a quiet chat on religious subjects, yet I should conclude that generally he was reserved on these matters. Never were they obtruded on the general company; and all that he said on those topics was said in that quiet unostentatious manner that impressed me with the feeling that there was in him a deep realising of eternity as closely connected with time.

No. II.

PACIFIC STEAM NAVIGATION COY.'S OFFICE,
LIVERPOOL, 21st Sept. 1869.

At a meeting of the Court of Directors held here this day, Mr Charles Turner, M.P., the Chairman of the Company, presiding, the recent death of Mr John Elder was brought under notice, and it was unanimously resolved that, having regard to the late Mr Elder's long and valued connection with the Company, a vote of condolence with Mrs Elder be recorded, that Mr Just communicate the same, and express the deep sympathy of the Directors with her under her severe and trying affliction.

PACIFIC STEAM NAVIGATION COY.,
LIVERPOOL, 21st Sept. 1869.

MY DEAR MRS ELDER,—It is now my duty to transmit herewith an extract from the minutes of the Board to-day, expressing the sincere sympathy of the Directors under your present trying dispensation ; and I feel it due, alike to the memory of your late respected husband and to the Directors, to add, that in his death they recognise the loss of a valued connection and private friend.—I remain, my dear Mrs Elder, yours very sincerely,

WILLIAM JUST.

Mrs ELDER, Elm Park, Govan, Glasgow.

PACIFIC STEAM NAVIGATION COMPANY,
HARRINGTON STREET, LIVERPOOL, 23d Nov. 1869.

Mrs ELDER, Elm Park, near Glasgow :

DEAR MADAM,—I am instructed by the Directors to inform you that they have this day unanimously resolved that, in recognition of your late husband's services to this Company, in the economy of fuel through the use of his compound engines, one of the vessels now building by the firm for the West Coast service should bear his name. The vessel last contracted for shall therefore be called the "John Elder."—I am, dear Madam, yours very truly,

WILLIAM JUST.

PACIFIC STEAM NAVIGATION COMPANY,
HARRINGTON STREET, LIVERPOOL, 21st Oct. 1870.

In reply to your inquiry as to the extent and nature of the Company's business connection with the late lamented John Elder, and with the firm of Messrs Randolph, Elder, & Co., of which he was the guiding spirit—so far as regards marine steam-engines, I may explain that it began in the year 1856, on the occasion of supplying to the Valparaiso a set of engines on Mr Elder's compound principle —the second, as I believe, of the class made by the firm; shipbuilding being subsequently added to the engineering business, which together were ultimately carried on by Mr Elder alone. The Company have built no fewer than

E

22 steam-ships in that yard, and have been supplied, including those now building, with 30 pairs of the double-cylindered engines. In fact, on account of the advantages in the saving of fuel, which, according to our experience, reaches 30 to 35 per cent, we would not think of any other type of machinery.

As you are no doubt aware, the operations have, up to a recent period, been confined to the west coast of South America, where, in consequence of the high price, economy of fuel is of the first importance. It was during the Russian war, when tonnage for the conveyance of coal hence to the Pacific became so scarce, and the cost of the article abroad was thereby more than doubled for a time, that we were led to inquire into the question of a saving of coal. Mr Elder was called in and consulted, and the double-cylinder engine adopted, as before mentioned, and with a success far beyond our most sanguine expectations, or the advantages held out by Mr Elder himself. Indeed I am in fairness bound to admit, that his double-cylinder engines never exceeded the promised consumption, nor fell short of the guaranteed speed. On the contrary, the promised results were always more than realised; and I may add, that such was the progress in improvement in the double-cylinder engines, that the last-delivered vessels surpassed the Valparaiso in the economy of fuel as far as she surpassed the ordinary type of machinery.

A short time before Mr Elder's death, the Company undertook to carry out a mail service for the Chili Government between Europe and Valparaiso, and he was called on to design and construct four large steam-ships of upwards of 3000 tons and 500 horse-power. Those vessels have been so remarkable as regards regularity in performance of the voyage, a distance of 19,000 miles on the round— the greatest steam-line in the world—and economical in the consumption of coal, that the attention of many large steam-ship owners, who had long remained sceptical, has been more particularly attracted to the merits of the compound engine, so that ere long I believe the old type of machinery will be unheard of. For this rapid stride in economy, steam-ship owners are, no doubt, indebted to Mr Elder ; and many successful lines of steamers have been projected which never would have had an existence but for the compound principle ; thus carrying out the great idea of not only bringing greater advantages and new pleasures into existence, but so cheapening those that previously existed as to bring them within the reach of many who otherwise could not have enjoyed them : and thus also will Mr Elder's name be transmitted to posterity as a worthy disciple of Watt.

. . . .

Speaking from long experience, I can aver that, whether in friendship or business, no man could have been more reliable, or more worthy of confidence.

WILLIAM JUST.

No. III.

INSTITUTION OF ENGINEERS IN SCOTLAND.
SECRETARY'S OFFICE, 67 RENFIELD STREET,
GLASGOW, 27th Sept. 1869.

Mr J. P. Smith begs herewith to transmit to Mrs Elder the enclosed excerpt minute of meeting of council of the Institution of Engineers, which he trusts she will kindly receive. He would at the same time desire to express his own sympathy.

THE INSTITUTION OF ENGINEERS IN SCOTLAND,
with which is incorporated
THE SCOTTISH SHIPBUILDERS' ASSOCIATION,
GLASGOW, 27th Sept. 1869.

(Excerpt of Minute of Council held on 3d Sept. 1869.)

It was unanimously resolved that the council of the Institution formally record their deep sense of the great loss the Institution had sustained by the death of their President, Mr John Elder, and also of the misfortune which had befallen the profession, in losing in the prime of life one whose skill, energy, and varied attainments had done so much for its advancement.

It was further resolved that the council transmit to Mrs Elder the expression of their sympathy in her bereavement, with the assurance that Mr Elder's memory will remain with them associated with all that is to be esteemed for high professional ability, integrity of purpose, and trustworthy friendship.

Extracted from the minutes.

J. P. SMITH,
Secretary.

No. IV.

BURGH CHAMBERS, GOVAN,
12th October 1869.

Mrs ELDER, Govan :

MADAM,—I have the melancholy satisfaction of transmitting to you the annexed excerpt from the minutes of the Police Commissioners of the Burgh of Govan.— I have the honour to be, Madam, your most obedient servant,

W. M. WILSON,
Burgh-Clerk.

" At Govan, and within the Burgh Chambers, the eleventh October 1869. At a general meeting of the Police Commissioners of the burgh, Provost Thomas Reid in the chair,—

" *Inter alia*, the Chairman officially reported the death since last meeting of John Elder, Esq., one of the Commissioners, and moved—' That the Commissioners resolve to record in their minutes that by the death of John Elder, Esq., their Board has been deprived of a member from whose presence, had health permitted it, and life been spared, their deliberations would have derived invaluable aid and enhanced authority ; and that the general community of the burgh honour the memory of a marine engineer of distinguished genius and enterprise, while they lament the loss of a large and beneficent employer of labour, a public-spirited citizen, and a good man ; and resolve further, that a copy of the minute be transmitted to Mrs Elder, with the respectful condolence of the Commissioners upon her irreparable bereavement.'

"The Commissioners unanimously approved of the Provost's motion, and instructed the clerk accordingly."

Extracted from the minutes by

W. M. WILSON,
Clerk.

No. V.

ASSOCIATION OF ENGINEERS IN GLASGOW.
GLASGOW, *17th Sept.* 1869.

Mrs ELDER :

DEAR MADAM, — In acknowledgment of Mr Elder's letter of the 7th Sept. last, accepting the honorary membership of this Association, I am directed by the council to express to you our deep sense of the loss we have sustained by his lamented death, and to express our very sincere sympathy with you in your heavy bereavement.— I am, Madam, your respectful and obedient servant.

WM. GEORGE BOWSER,
Secy., Session 1868-69.

ELM PARK.

No. VI.

*Extract from Letter of W. Edward MacAndrew, Esq.,
of Messrs MacAndrew & Co.*

BOND COURT CHAMBERS,
WALBROOK, LONDON, *Oct.* 22, 1870.

. . . .

In all, we had ten steamers built, and three more engined—thirteen in all—by Mr Elder. I believe that he built his first screw-steamer for us, and she is still running with most satisfactory results—indeed, our unparalleled success in the steam business, in face of severe opposition, is solely attributable to our connection with Mr Elder enabling us to effect such economies over our opponents.

Mr Elder was our consulting engineer as well as the contractor for the work, and everything that he could personally superintend was uniformly successful in its results.

. . . .

Both Mr Elder and myself were animated by a desire to introduce improvements and economies into naval architecture and marine engineering; and it was a knowledge of Mr Elder's views in this matter which led to our seeking him in the first place. We joined in experiments, which naturally cost something at first, but were ultimately very successful and pecuniarily advantageous to both firms. . . . I know that had he lived, he would have introduced, at least, as great reforms into naval as into mercantile building and engineering.

I have only to add that Mr Elder was always most

liberal in all matters of contract, and by his constant ur-
banity and liberal execution of all contracts, commanded
a preference over all other builders. His personal work
and superintendence were hardly less valuable to the business than his irresistible courtesy and unmistakable intelli-
gence in going into any matter.

   .   .   .   .

He was always ready to give his time to discussing any
suggestion, whether made by himself or others, and was
not only thoroughly scientific, but eminently practical.
Unlike other inventors, he did not overstate results to be
attained, nor did he press his inventions on those who
were too prejudiced to adopt them. He built steamers
and engines of the old style for those who so wished
them, and always laid the case fairly before his customers.
. . . Naturally, old plans and old ways are preferred by many, and few *could* move as fast as Mr Elder
in evolving or executing improved systems.

   .   .   .   .

W. Edward MacAndrew.

No. VII.

*Extract from Letter of H. Oliver Robinson, Esq., contrac-
tor for the Dutch East Indian Steam-Packet Service.*

Edinburgh, 26th October 1870.

   .   .   .   .

This service (I may explain) embraces six lines of inter-
colonial steam-navigation, centring at Batavia, the capital,

performing regular voyages to and from the following ports : Singapore (connecting with the European lines), Samarang, Sourabaya, and Cheribon, in Java ; Padang, Bencoolen, and Palembang, in Sumatra; Macassar and Menado, in Celebes ; Amboyna, Banda, and Ternate, in the Spice Islands; Sinkawang and Bandjermassing, in Borneo; and requiring for the performance of this service at least ten steam-vessels of different sizes or classes.

Those steam-vessels were required to be specially adapted for a tropical climate, and for seas where "fouling" takes place with a rapidity far exceeding those of a temperate climate ; whilst the high cost of coals (about £2 per ton) rendered economy of consumption of the first importance.

When to these conditions is added the shallowness of the coasts, the prevalence of coral reefs and sandbanks, and the absence of lighthouses and beacons in this Eastern Archipelago, it will be readily understood that steam-vessels of a highly special adaptation were indispensable to success, both in a maritime and financial point of view.

It is unnecessary for me here to refer to the acquaintance I had previously the pleasure to form with Mr Elder, beyond saying that from it I felt the conviction that he possessed in a high degree the talents and experience necessary to aid me in designing those steam-vessels, and in determining the leading points in the construction of the vessels and engines.

To him accordingly, upon my return from Java in

August 1864, I, as the contractor with the Dutch Colonial
Government for this steam-service, applied for this aid;
and, with his well-known generosity and kindness, he
threw himself unsparingly into the subject, and by our
joint labours the working drawings and specifications of
the whole of the necessary steam-vessels, with their machinery and boilers, were finally settled.

The relative importance of those different lines of steam-
navigation necessarily determined the sizes and powers of
the steam-vessels, and *three* classes were fixed upon as
follows, viz. :—

First class, 1050 tons builders' measurement, and 200
horses' power.

Second class, 850 tons builders' measurement, and 150
horses' power.

Third class, 500 tons builders' measurement, and 80
horses' power.

From the fact that all the ten steam-vessels were required to be out at Batavia ready to commence the service
on the 1st January 1866, Mr Elder's firm could only
undertake to build and engine four, and to engine a fifth
steamer, being all of the first and second class; and accordingly, contracts for their delivery "ready for sea" at
certain fixed dates were entered into with the firm, and
were duly and faithfully performed; and on the trial, the
speed and consumption of coals completely fulfilled the
stipulated conditions.

These steam-vessels have now been running nearly five
years, without any perceptible falling-off, and without re-

quiring repairs to either vessels, machinery, or boilers—
the only matter of regret being that the whole of the fleet
could not have been obtained from the same source.

It may be of interest to refer here to a few of the peculiar points of those steam-vessels, which were considered
necessary to adapt them to the service in question.

Their draught light, with great beam. The passen-
ger accommodation all on deck, spacious and airy, covered
by a spar deck. The rig schooner, with taunt masts,
and large canvas for the light winds of the Eastern
Archipelago, where typhoons never reach. But the
engines were more especially the point to which Mr
Elder devoted his attention, and on which he showed the
great liberality of his mind.

Owing to the circumstances that those steamers never
would have occasion to return to Europe in the ordinary
course, and that the Suez Canal was *then* not a fact, it was
obviously desirable to have their engines and boilers of
the most simple design, whilst the light construction of
the vessels rendered it of importance to keep down the
weight of the machinery as much as possible. To meet
these desiderata, single-cylinder engines of the most
economical possible consumption, instead of his own
double-cylinder engines, were proposed to him by me.
This idea he at once entered into, and applied himself to
the carrying of it out with his usual ardour, and with
such success, that upon the trial-trips of the steamers the
consumption of *Scotch* coal was only 2¾ lb. per horse-
power per hour (indicated).

In all these matters of engineering and construction, the only partner of the firm with whom I came in contact was Mr Elder, whom, in addition to his great talents and liberal views in mechanical matters, I found to be exceedingly straightforward, as well as easy to deal with on all financial points.

.   .   .   .

H. OLIVER ROBINSON.

No. VIII.

LEITH, 3d *November* 1870.

.   .   .   .

I had been some time groping after some method of getting better results from the marine engine, when I became acquainted with Mr Elder, and at once saw he had thoroughly mastered the whole question. I have had seven pairs of those engines, all working now in the most perfect order, and giving the most complete satisfaction.

When I saw the results of the first pair, I ventured to predict that they must entirely supersede all other marine engines; and I am now seeing them adopted by those who were keenest in depreciation of them.

The vessels in which my engines were placed are doing their work in all parts of the world, and doing it well. Nearly all of them have been trading to the East, *viâ* the Suez Canal; and no one can doubt that Mr Elder's invention has placed steam-navigation on a footing which will enable it, by means of the Canal, to extend indefinitely commerce and civilisation in the East.

It was a true pleasure to have business dealings with Mr Elder, as it was a true happiness to enjoy his private friendship. I had to send no inspector to see work faithfully done in an establishment where all work was faithfully done. Mr Elder was ever ready to give information and advice; and my experience has invariably been that I obtained in practice *better* results than promised, a somewhat unusual experience of inventors. I often told Mr Elder I wished I had known him sooner. It would have been well for the world had he been spared to us longer.

.   .   .   .

DONALD R. MACGREGOR.

No. IX.

Letter on part of Employees.

FAIRFIELD YARD, *Sept.* 20, 1869.

MY DEAR SIR,—The employees of our late deceased employer, Mr Elder, are desirous of showing their gratitude, and the manner in which they esteem his memory, by being granted the liberty of following his remains to the place of interment, or part of the way, in whatever manner the relations of our late worthy employer shall see fit to appoint. They will feel grateful by this boon being granted them, as it may be the last open mark that they shall have the liberty of ascribing to his memory, and their sympathy towards his bereaved wife and relations.—Your obedient servant,

ALEXANDER NEIL.

Mr LORIMER.

No. X.

Letter on the part of Foremen and Workmen.

GOVAN, 22d Sept. 1869.

DEAR MADAM,—At a meeting of the Fairfield Accident Fund Committee (representing the entire body of the foremen and workmen in Fairfield Shipbuilding Yard) it was unanimously resolved to address to you a letter of condolence expressing our sentiments of heartfelt sympathies with you in being bereaved of your loving spouse, and ourselves deprived of a deservingly - esteemed employer.

We would refrain from intruding upon your acute grief at this time, but our feelings constrain us to give unqualified expression to our sincere grief for the irreparable loss which you have sustained.

By this sad calamity we mourn the loss of the most benevolent of employers and the most generous of masters —the community the loss of the enterprising and important supporter—the benevolent and the Christian that material aid which enabled them to make provision for the needy—the erring restrained and advised towards a new life.

By this sad calamity we mourn the loss as a star of the first magnitude in the engineering and shipbuilding system which has suddenly vanished, but whose lustre shall outlive the present generation.

By this sad calamity Scotland has cause to weep for an ingenious and illustrious son, rearing a memorial in the hearts of the people which shall remain untarnished during succeeding ages.

And now that we have confidence that he has gone to his rest, we earnestly desire that this providential visitation may be sanctified to you and to us; may God the Father be to you the husband of the widow, your stay and protector in all circumstances—God the Son your friend and adviser—and God the Holy Spirit your comforter in your sad bereavement, is the prayer of your sincere sympathisers and faithful servants,

ALEXR. NEIL, *President,*

WM. MILLAR, *Secretary*

for the Fairfield Accident Fund Committee.

To Mrs JOHN ELDER.

THE END.

www.ingramcontent.com/pod-product-compliance
Lightning Source LLC
Chambersburg PA
CBHW020047030726
47499CB00007B/2632